◄I'M GOING TO BE A►

Police Officer

12.99

◄I'M GOING TO BE A►
Police
Officer

by Edith Kunhardt

The author thanks Dave, Cindi, David Jr., and Michelle Griffiths for their kind help and cooperation despite busy schedules and round-the-clock duties. Sincere thanks also to Chief Glen Stonemetz, Jr., and to other members of the East Hampton Village Police Department, East Hampton, N.Y., for their willingness to participate in this book.

ISBN 0-590-25485-5

Copyright © 1995 by Edith Kunhardt.
All rights reserved. Published by Scholastic Inc.
CARTWHEEL BOOKS and the CARTWHEEL BOOKS logo are registered trademarks of Scholastic Inc.

12 11 10 9 8 7 6 5 4 3 2 1   5 6 7 8 9/9 0/0

Printed in the U.S.A.   24

First Scholastic printing, September 1995

J363.2
KUN

Cartwheel
·B·O·O·K·S· ®

SCHOLASTIC INC.

New York   Toronto   London   Auckland   Sydney

My name is Michelle. This is my mom. This is my dad and my big brother, David. We live in this house.

My dad is a police officer. I want to be a police officer when I grow up. David wants to be one, too.

In the morning, Dad puts on his police uniform.
He puts on his bulletproof vest. The vest is made of
tightly woven material to protect him.

He wears a shirt over the vest. His holster and revolver, handcuffs, whistle, and handcuff key are attached to his belt.

Today David and I are
going to visit Daddy at the
police station. We ride to
the station in his police
car.

We say hello to the chief.

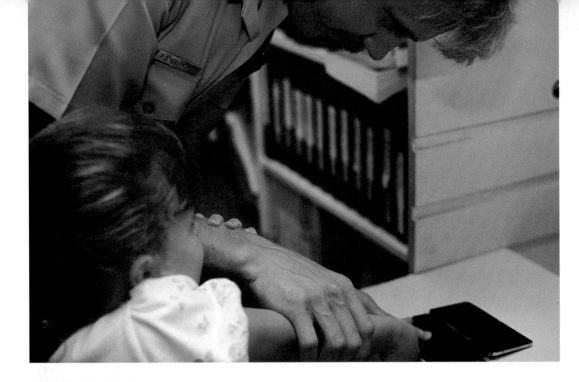

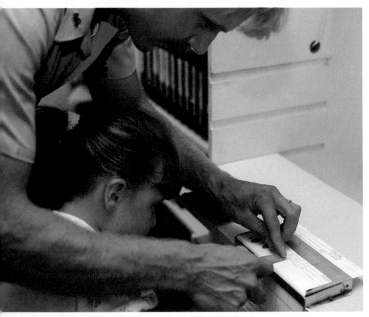

I'm getting fingerprinted. Dad pushes my fingers onto an ink pad. Then he presses them onto a white card.

Pretty soon my fingerprints are all done.

David gets fingerprinted, too. Then he looks at the "Most Wanted" poster.

There is a jail in the police station. The jail is just one room. No one is in it now. When there is a prisoner in the jail, a light inside stays on all night and a television camera watches the prisoner.

Dad works at the desk. An emergency call comes in. Someone is sick.

Dad calls a patrol car and tells the driver where to go to bring help.

Before I go home, I give Daddy the lunch that we packed for him.

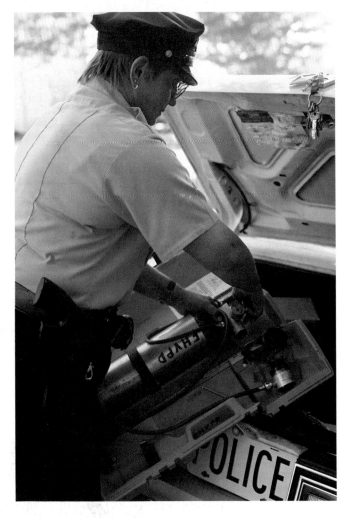

Later, Dad sees Officer Maxey. She is checking the oxygen equipment in a police car.

She uses her walkie-talkie.

Dad patrols the town. He knows everybody.

A traffic officer marks a car and the road with her chalk stick. She'll come back in an hour. If the mark on the tire and the mark on the road still line up, the car has been parked too long.

Then she writes a ticket.

Later, Dad sees the officer directing traffic.

Dad uses a radar gun to check for speeders. He points the gun at a car, and the gun registers how fast the car is going. That car is going 25 miles an hour. It's not speeding.

Dad makes notes in his book. Then a call comes in on his special car radio.

"Lost dog on Gingerbread Lane," says a voice from headquarters.

"Ten-four," says Dad. That means "message received."

Dad drives to Gingerbread Lane. There's the lost dog. Dad gets out of his car.

"Come here, old boy," he says.

Dad reads the dog's license number. He writes it down on his pad. Dad takes the dog to the pound, where the dog's owner can pick him up.

Sometimes Dad works all night. He patrols the streets. He checks the doors of stores to see if they're locked.

Uh-oh, this door opens. A burglar alarm goes off! Is there a burglar inside? No.

Daddy goes into the store to see if everything is all right. Someone from the alarm company will come to turn off the alarm.

Mommy picks me and David up after school. Sometimes Daddy is at the school crossing. He stops the traffic so we can cross the street.

We're going home. Oh! Oh! Stop the car. Someone has had an accident. It's our friend, Chris. He fell off his bike.

Dad calls the ambulance. Soon Chris's leg is bandaged.

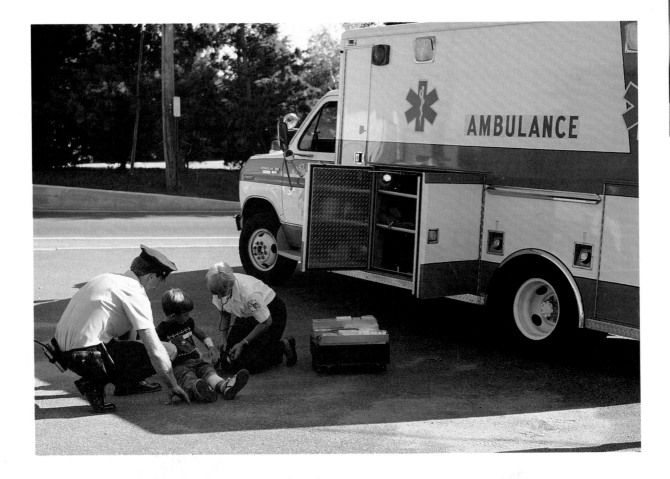

"Do you want to come in?" asks the ambulance driver. We go inside.

It's fun inside the ambulance. Chris has his blood pressure taken. He feels fine. Then we go home.

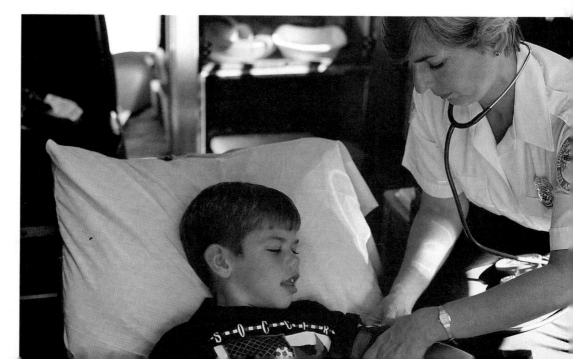

My dad is busy. He helps
people and protects people.

I'm going to be a police officer.